S
Th

Home Farm Twins

Sunny
The Hero

Jenny Oldfield
Illustrated by Kate Aldous

*Hodder
Children's
Books*

a division of Hodder Headline plc

A Catalogue record for this book is available from the British Library

ISBN 0 340 68990 0

Typeset by Avon Dataset Ltd, Bidford-on-Avon, Warks

Printed and bound in Great Britain by
Mackays of Chatham PLC, Chatham, Kent

Hodder Children's Books
a division of Hodder Headline plc
338 Euston Road
London NW1 3BH

One

'This little piggy went to market . . .'

Helen and Hannah Moore sat in the front room at Home Farm and stared at their father. Baby Joe Stott sat like a roly-poly dumpling on David Moore's knee, loving every second of the jiggling rhyme.

'*This* little piggy stayed at home.

'*This* little piggy had roast beef!'

Joe squirmed and chuckled as the twins' dad grabbed each of his toes.

'And *this* little piggy had none.'

Helen bit deep into a home-made flapjack, still staring at her dad. She glanced at Hannah as if to say,

'He's gone a bit over the top with the ga-ga, goo-goo baby bit, hasn't he?' But Hannah's face was one big, shiny smile.

'And *this* little piggy cried "Wee, wee, wee!"

All the way home!'

Joe giggled and wriggled on their father's lap. Julie Stott, the baby's mother, sat on the sofa next to him, cooing away. Joe lifted his fat arms to her and she went and scooped him up. But as soon as she held him he squawked to be free. Julie set him down on the rug and let him crawl towards Hannah and Helen. He came on all fours, gurgling happily.

'Isn't he sweet?' Hannah breathed, her voice soft and sugary.

Sweet? Helen nearly choked. First her dad – now her twin sister! As far as she was concerned, babies were messy creatures. You never knew what they were going to do next.

Joe sat back on his haunches and popped his wet lips at them. He stared up at Helen's flapjack with his big blue eyes.

'What does he want?' Helen whispered out of the corner of her mouth.

'He wants you to give him some of that.' Hannah

clapped her hands for him to keep on crawling.

Helen sat back with a frown. If Joe Stott had been a puppy or a kitten, a pony or a fluffy lamb, that would have been different. She would have given him the whole biscuit.

'No, Joe, you've just had your dinner.' His father, Dan, came and picked him up. Dan Stott was huge, well over six feet tall. He had curly, golden-red hair, grey eyes and freckles. Joe was a mini version of his dad – small and round, with the same hair, but those big blue eyes. 'We only called in to ask you along to the show tomorrow, this being your first summer in Doveton.'

Helen and Hannah's mother, Mary, stepped forward. The whole house was warm from the heat of the oven, and smells of baking wafted through from the kitchen. She ran a small café in Nesfield, but tonight was her Big Bake for the summer show. It took place in the fields behind the cricket pitch at the foot of Doveton Fell. There would be two big striped tents for flower displays and food stalls, and pens filled with sheep, cows, pigs and goats all hoping to win a rosette for the best of their breed. There would be children's races and sheepdog displays. And best of all, the twins' mum would set up a cake stall and

Helen and Hannah would help to run it. They could hardly wait.

'That's kind of you, Dan.' Mary Moore smiled and gave Joe's podgy feet a gentle tickle. 'But we already know about the show. It's the biggest event of the year, isn't it?'

The young farmer's freckled face flushed bright red. 'Well, we wanted you to feel at home. It was Julie's idea. She knows how it feels to be new to the village.'

Before she'd met and married Dan, Julie's home had been in Manchester. She'd swapped the big city for Clover Farm, a job with computers for life as a farmer's wife and mother of baby Joe. 'It can be hard to make friends,' she admitted. 'So we wanted to make you welcome.'

Mary laughed. 'We already feel we've lived here all our lives, don't we, girls?'

They nodded. Helen had gobbled her flapjack and felt much happier now that Joe was safe in his dad's arms.

'When we first came the house did feel a bit empty and run-down, but Hannah and Helen soon filled it with animals. They're mad keen on anything with four legs.'

'We've got Speckle!' Hannah reached to stroke the young sheepdog's head. He pricked up his ears at the sound of his name.

'And Solo!' Hannah was proud of their grey pony, who had come to Home Farm after they'd worked so hard to buy him.

'And goats, geese, rabbits and chickens!' Helen gabbled.

'Last time I looked, geese and chickens only had *two* legs,' David Moore grinned.

'You know what I mean, Dad!' Hannah loved everything about their new life in the Lake District, but especially their collection of pets at Home Farm.

'We haven't got a cat – so far!' Helen reminded them. She let them know she was working on this one. 'Have *you*?' she asked Dan Stott eagerly.

'Not a spare one.' He grinned down at her. 'We've got Martha at Clover Farm, but she's getting on a bit. She's an old lady now.'

Helen's face fell and she sighed.

'We don't keep many animals at the farm.' Dan explained that he'd recently taken over from his uncle. Clover Farm was in the valley at the far end of the lake. They grew crops like wheat and vegetables.

'But we do keep a few pigs,' he told them. 'To eat up the waste. Large whites.'

'Large what?' Hannah's ears pricked up.

'Whites. It's a breed of pigs. We have a boar called Duke and two sows called Queenie and Princess.'

'And piglets?' Hannah wanted to know.

'Steady on,' her father warned. He knew what that look in her eye meant.

'Lots. I rear them to show, then I sell them on to other breeders. Some of my pigs are country champions!' he said proudly as he handed baby Joe to Julie and the family got ready to leave.

'Large Whites,' Hannah repeated. 'What do they look like?'

'They're not really white at all. They're pale pink with sticky-up ears, not flop-ears,' Dan went on to explain. 'The sow has ten piglets per litter, but often she'll only rear eight or nine—'

'You can see them tomorrow,' Julie broke in. Baby Joe had his jump suit zipped up and his mini-trainers laced. He made hungry noises and shoved his fist into his mouth. 'When you come to the show,' she finished.

'Try and stop them,' Mary smiled. 'They'll be

helping me on my stall, but there'll be plenty of time to look round too.'

'Yes, come and see Princess. Queenie won't be there because she has to stay home and look after her piglets. But Princess and Duke will.' Dan had picked up his wife's hint and made for the door.

'I'll take some photographs,' David promised. It was his job to shoot pictures of animals for newspapers and magazines. It needed patience and a very good camera. David Moore had both.

'We'll help!' Hannah offered.

'Great. Let's hope it stays fine.' Dan Stott stood on the doorstep and looked up at the pink evening sky.

The twins followed their visitors out into the farmyard. The honeysuckle climbing up a side wall gave off a strong, sweet smell. Speckle bounded ahead, ready for his walk. The glossy brown chickens scratched for food by the gate, Solo came from the next-door paddock and put his head over the wall to check on the strangers as their car drove away.

Helen and Hannah watched it go, then slowly climbed the stile with Speckle to set off up the fell. The shadows fell long and thin across the steep valley. Down below, Doveton Lake shone silver-grey. The

twins turned to look at the big, round show-tents by the waterside. From here they looked like striped toy roundabouts at a fair.

'Pigs,' Hannah said thoughtfully. She watched Helen throw a stick for Speckle.

'They smell,' Helen reminded her. Babies; pigs; somehow they got mixed up in her mind. Both were pink and squidgy, smelly and fat.

'No more than other animals.'

'Hmm.' Doubtfully Helen walked on.

'A nice pinky-white piglet,' Hannah dreamed on. Something new for Home Farm; a squeaking, grunting, roly-poly sweet little piglet.

Tomorrow they would meet Princess and make friends with one of Dan Stott's prize Large White sows. After that they might visit the farm to see the Stotts' latest litter of piglets. And then . . . who knew what would happen?

Two

Speckle wove in and out of the farmers' legs at Doveton Show. They stood round the pens where the judges in white coats marked their sheep, leaning on the fences and pointing out why their own sturdy ewe should win first prize.

'Now then,' John Fox grumbled at Speckle as the dog pushed by. But he made room for him to say hello to his own dog, Ben. Then he turned to Helen and Hannah. 'Have you saved me one of your mother's fruit cakes like I asked?'

'The biggest one,' Helen promised. 'Did your sheep win a prize?'

11

'Aye, the blue ribbon for that shearling over there.' Old Mr Fox pointed to one of his own young ewes. He gave a gap-toothed grin. 'And I'll soon be putting Ben through his paces at the sheepdog trials.' It was a busy day for him and for all the Lake District farmers who'd brought their animals to the show.

Speckle ran on to the next pen. Here the judges were picking out the best goat, and it was another of Helen and Hannah's friends who won the first prize. They watched proudly as the judge came over to shaken Len Coates by the hand.

'Sheba's a fine little goat,' she told him, 'with a lovely glossy coat and an intelligent head. That's what I like to see.'

The twins glowed with pride for Len. They knew that each and every one of his goats at Skrike Farm were beautifully looked after. So far the sunny show day was turning out even better than expected.

The twins had been up with the lark. They'd loaded boxes of cakes, buns, scones and biscuits into the Curlew Café van and driven down to the show-field with their mum. They'd found their cake stall inside one of the big striped tents, next to a jam and pickle stall on one side and flower arrangements on the other. They'd spread their long table with a red and white checked cloth, then arranged their cakes ready for the rush.

At ten o'clock the gates had opened and people poured in. There were farmers in tweed jackets and caps, tourists in bright T-shirts and shorts. There was Mr Saunders from Doveton Manor standing on a platform to open the show, and everyone from the village. Luke Martin was nearby with an ice-cream stall. Miss Wesley, the twins' teacher, was on hand to help. Then there were friends from school trying to buy cakes at bargain prices, and fussy Mr Winter scolding his dog, Puppy, for gobbling up the crumbs.

'Tired?' Mary Moore asked the twins just before lunch. The showground was packed out, the loud-speaker announcing that judging the pigs was about to begin.

Hannah nodded. She pushed her dark fringe from her hot face.

'Have another break,' her mum suggested. 'Your dad can take over here for a while.'

'I can?' David Moore panicked. 'I just came by to see how you were getting on.' His camera was slung round his neck, his shirt sleeves were rolled up and

13

his wavy brown hair was ruffled by the wind.

Mary grabbed him quickly. 'Let the girls go for a walk around,' she insisted. 'It's easy to serve the cakes. There's nothing to it. This one here's carrot. This one's pecan nuts and syrup, this is Dundee fruit cake . . .'

Hannah and Helen made their getaway. They ducked under the table and wove between the crowded stalls until their dad called them back.

'Uh-oh!' Hannah warned. She was tired of serving cakes and she wanted to see the pigs.

Helen turned and dragged her feet back to the stall.

'Take some pictures,' he said, handing her his camera. 'I promised Dan Stott, remember?'

Helen said she would do her best, then went to join Speckle and Hannah outside the main tent.

'How do we find the pig competition?' Hannah couldn't see over the top of the crowd.

'Just follow our noses, I expect.' Helen sniffed. 'We should be able to smell them a mile off.'

'Ho, ho.' Hannah wasn't amused by the smelly pig joke.

They picked their way slowly towards a cluster of people gathered round a small arena where the pigs were to be shown. Speckle wagged his tail and lay down in the sun. Helen held her nose.

Hannah leaned on the white fence, amazed. There were pink pigs and black pigs, pink-and-black pigs and hairy brown pigs. Every one of them was scrubbed clean and brushed to a silky shine. The judges stood in a knot in the middle of the circle, muttering about Landraces and Saddlebacks and Gloucester Old Spots.

'There's Princess,' said a deep voice just to one side of the twins.

They turned to look up. It was Dan Stott, standing with his freckled arms folded, nodding proudly towards a huge pink pig with a fat face and hairy ears. Her mouth curled up at the corners and her tiny eyes almost vanished behind folds of flesh.

'Her real name is Princess of Cumbria,' Dan told them. 'Pure Large White, weighs in at nearly four hundred kilograms. I have high hopes for Princess today.' He stared anxiously as the judges moved in to study her.

'Quick!' Hannah jabbed Helen with her elbow. 'Take some pictures!'

Helen took her fingers from her nose, but she still

tried not to breathe through it. She held the camera to her eye and pressed the shutter just too late. Princess raised her head, snorted and turned her broad back.

'Did you get it?' Hannah whispered.

'*Doh*.'

'No?'

'*Doh*.' Helen put her hand back over her nose.

'Look out, she's coming across!' Hannah cried.

The pig turned again. Her mouth open, double-chins wobbling, she lumbered towards them. Dan stood head and shoulders above the crowd, and Princess had spotted him.

Click – click – click! Helen took action shots. *Snort – snort – grunt*! Princess broke into a thunderous trot. The crowd stepped back nervously as she headed for the fence.

'Look out!' Dan pushed to the front and vaulted into the ring. He stood his ground as Princess charged. 'There, steady on, girl.' He seized a wooden board which was propped nearby and held it out to steer the sow away from the fence. 'That's it, calm down. You're not going anywhere.' Waiting for her to stop, Dan looked as though he were a match for even a four hundred kilogram pig. Sure enough, Princess

16

shuddered to a halt and came snuffling up. Dan scratched her head. The crowd heaved a sigh of relief.

'Well, I don't like the look of that,' Helen and Hannah heard one of the judges mutter.

The rest shook their heads and tutted.

Having calmed Princess, Dan climbed out of the ring. 'That's torn it.' He seemed upset. 'It looked much worse than it was, as it happens. Princess is over-friendly, that's her trouble.' He knew now that he wouldn't be going home with a blue rosette.

'Never mind, Helen took some good pictures,' Hannah told him.'

'And we've still got Duke to come in the boar section,' Dan said. 'He stands a good chance of third prize at least.'

And when the twins finally saw Duke they under-stood why. If Princess was four hundred kilos of solid pink muscle, Duke must weigh in at at least five hundred. The boar was massive, his face whiskery, his tail curled and tufted. His bottom lip jutted out, his broad snout sprouted thick white hairs. As he came into the ring, he waddled and swayed, squinting out through his tiny piggy eyes.

'Wow!' Hannah breathed.

17

'Oh, *doh*!' Helen couldn't believe the size of him.

'The Duke of Doveton,' Dan announced. 'And I'd like to see a pig round here that can beat that!'

It took the judges half an hour to agree. They gave the yellow rosette to a rough, tough Saddleback from a farm near Nesfield, and the red second prize rosette to a flop-eared Landrace from over the fell. But the prize and the blue rosette went to the magnificent Duke of Doveton from Clover Farm. He won the major prize-money and a huge round of applause.

It was Hannah's turn to take the photographs: Duke with the blue rosette clipped to his ear, Duke with rosette and Dan, Duke with rosette, Dan, Julie and baby Joe. Hannah clicked until the film ran out.

'Congratulations!' David Moore came to find them after his spell of helping out on the cake stall. The sun was still hot, and the crowd were looking for shade and a cool drink. 'I heard them announce the prizes over the loudspeaker. Well done, Dan. You must be very pleased.'

He blushed. 'Well, the money will come in handy,' he confessed.

'It's the pigs that helps to keep us going at Clover

Sunny The Hero

Farm,' Julie added. 'And now that Duke's won the blue ribbon, his piglets will be worth more too.' She smiled, while Joe gurgled from underneath his white sunhat.

'He's certainly a magnificent animal.' David Moore stood watching, hands in his pockets, as Dan went to round Duke up, ready to lead him into a trailer parked nearby.

Hannah went and took a peek inside. Princess was already there, grunting happily in her bed of straw.

'Not keen on pigs, eh?' David asked Helen. She hung back with Speckle at the ringside.

'*Doh. Dasty, doisy*, dirty things!' she snuffled.

'What's the matter? Have you got hayfever?'

'*Doh*. My *dose* is blocked.' She'd held it so hard to block out the smell of pigs that she was afraid she might have bunged it up for good.

Her dad grinned at her funny face. 'Here, have a tissue.'

She blew her nose loudly and breathed in fresh air. Gazing round, she sniffed again. 'That's funny.'

'What is?' Hannah had come back to join them now that Duke was safely in the trailer with Princess.

'There's no smell!'

Hannah tutted. 'What did I tell you? Pigs aren't any worse than other animals, are they, Dad?' She stood, shoulders back, hands on hips, daring him to disagree.

'Erm,' he coughed. On the other side of him Helen willed him to agree with her. 'Do pigs smell? That's the ten thousand dollar question, is it? He looked from one to the other.

'Yes!' They stared up at him.

'Well, let's develop the photographs, then you can take them over to Clover Farm tomorrow. You'll see for yourselves, won't you?'

'I'll take my gas-mask!' Helen threatened, still convinced that she was right.

'You won't need it,' Hannah retorted. 'It's all a big lie!'

Speckle gave one sharp bark.

'See, Speckle agrees!' Hannah turned and marched off towards the tent. 'Next to sheepdogs, pigs are just about the cleverest, cleanest animals around!'

Three

That evening Hannah worked in the darkroom with her dad, while Helen rode Solo out on the fell. The attic was warm and quiet. The small sloping window was blacked out, the shelves arranged with jars of photographic chemicals and paper.

'Here comes Princess!' Hannah peered into a square dish of clear liquid as the picture formed on the white paper. They worked by the light of a special red lamp so that the photographs could develop safely. 'See, she was charging towards Helen when she took the photo.'

The shape of the pig grew clear; ears pricked, head

up and mouth open as she ran at full gallop.

'That's a very good action shot,' David Moore said with a smile. He took the photograph out of the dish and hung it up to drip dry.

There were more of Princess taken by Helen, then the ones take by Hannah of Duke with his blue rosette – happy family photos of prize pig and proud owners.

'The pig looks as if he's smiling on this one,' Hannah's dad pointed out, 'as if he knows he's having his picture taken.'

'He probably does.' Hannah reminded him how clever pigs were. 'He's amazing, isn't he? I feel as if he could talk!'

'They're not that clever.' David Moore began to clear away the sour-smelling chemicals while Hannah checked the prints to see if they were dry.

'Want to bet?' She hummed as they cleaned and left the darkroom in good order. The photos had turned out well, and tomorrow, Sunday, the twins would take them to the Stotts' farm. Hannah went to bed dreaming of pigs. Clay pigs that she could model in art class at school, sugar pigs that she could buy from Luke Martin's shop, and real pigs running through fields of buttercups and clover. Little piglets scampering towards her, squeaking and squealing, or snuggled up snoring beside their mother.

'Do I really want to do this?' Helen asked out loud. They'd rushed breakfast, then run up to the attic to collect the pig photographs. Mary Moore said they should cycle down to Clover Farm with them, so now the twins were speeding down the lane into Doveton village. There was no one around on the fresh, breezy morning. Most people were still in bed after their hectic day at the show.

'Of course you do.' Hannah rode ahead through the empty main street. Puppy, Mr Winter's terrier, yapped at them from behind his garden gate, and Luke's white doves fluttered from the ground on to the roof of the village stores. 'Once you see how sweet piglets are, you'll soon change your mind.'

'I will?'

'Course.'

'But they grow so . . . big!' Helen rode over a bump and shot out of her saddle. 'Look at the size of Princess and Duke. They must eat a ton of food a day!'

Hannah laughed.

'OK, so not quite that much. But listen, Hannah,

you're not actually thinking of having one at Home Farm, are you?' The idea suddenly struck her – of course, this was the very thing that her sister *was* thinking.

Hannah's brown eyes sparkled as they rode their bikes past Lakeside Farm, out along the flat, narrow road that clung to the water's edge. Clover Farm was at the far end of the lane, a dead-end with hardly any traffic and a green, overgrown feel to the hedges and banks.

Helen's own eyes narrowed. 'Oh, no, Hannah!' Normally the twins saw eye to eye about animals. They might argue about schoolwork and who should do the washing-up, but they were both animal mad. But not about pigs! If Helen admitted the truth, she felt a bit scared of them, with their sharp little trotters and wide snouts, their sneaky little eyes and huge bodies. 'Anyway, Mum and Dad would never let us,' she added.

Hannah hummed a tune. '*This* little piggy went to market!' she sang. '*This* little piggy stayed at home . . .'

When she wanted, Hannah could be stubborn as a mule, Helen thought. Now a donkey: a lovely, furry, friendly donkey . . . that would be a better idea. A donkey in the paddock with Solo and their two young goat kids, Snip and Snap. Helen began to hum her own tune as Clover Farm came into view: 'Little donkey, little donkey, with your precious load . . . Gotta keep on, little donkey . . . de-dah-daah-da-da!'

Clover Farm was a pretty grey house built of Lakeland stone. It had roses rambling up the walls, and doors and windows open to the morning sun. There was a tractor in the yard and the sound of someone whistling inside the barn. An old grey cat came to meet the twins as they propped their bikes at the gate.

'You must be Martha.' Helen bent to stroke her. The cat purred and rubbed against her legs. So far, so good. There were no pig sounds or smells coming from the barn. She risked taking a deep breath and a look around.

Hannah ran straight to the barn. 'Hello?' she called. She held the envelope of photos tight in her hand.

Dan Stott soon came striding out. He saw the envelope and guessed why they'd come. 'That was quick.' He wiped his hands on his jeans and took the packet. 'Which do you want to do first; come inside for a cold drink, or out into the field to look at the piglets?'

'Drink!' Helen said.

'Piglets!' Hannah was even quicker.

'Come on then.' Dan put the photographs on a ledge and led the way.

Hannah followed eagerly, while Helen lagged behind. She sniffed the air – still so far, so good.

'I keep the pigs outdoors in the summer,' the farmer explained. 'They can rootle about and lie in the sun. And of course there's no mucking out for Julie and me to do, like there would be if we kept them indoors.

'And no smell?' Helen asked. They'd turned a corner behind the house and were climbing a stile over a high stone wall.

'Not much.' Dan jumped down first into the field. 'Not with a small herd like ours. Mind where you put your feet, though.'

Hannah jumped after him and landed safely. She looked round. The field ran on a slope down to the lake, fenced on all four sides by the ancient greeny-grey stone walls. At the high end of the flower-filled field she saw three metal huts. They were low and long, with round roofs.

'Those are the pigs' arks,' Dan said, striding up the hill, 'where they shelter if it rains. But today they should be out and about.'

'Come on!' Hannah turned to wait for Helen.

Hannah jumped and landed with a squelch.

'Trust you!' Hannah sighed.

'Yuk!' She scraped the sole of her shoe against a sharp stone. The smell she'd been dreading hit her nostrils.

Hannah grinned and left her to it. She ran after Dan Stott.

'This is Queenie's ark,' he told her. 'She'll be in there with her piglets. Duke and Princess are up by the hawthorn bushes, see.'

Hannah glanced at the two grown-up pigs nosing for food round the roots of the small trees. But it was piglets she had really come to see. She bent down to look through the entrance to the ark into the shady interior.

There was big fat Queenie lying on her side, legs stretched out, head towards them. She blinked and snorted when she saw Hannah, but she didn't move. Then Hannah saw the piglets: three, four, five of them all lined up in a row, suckling to their hearts' content.

Six, seven, eight: Queenie was feeding eight greedy piglets all at once! They pushed and shoved for the best place, some on top of others, the biggest ones struggling to get a teat near to the front of the sow, leaving the hind ones to their smaller brothers and sisters.

'Oh!' Hannah was speechless. The piglets were pink and tiny, wriggly and squirmy. And there were so many of them. She heard Helen come up from behind. 'Look at their tails,' she whispered. They waggled with pleasure as the piglets fed.

'Why aren't they curly?' Helen asked. Their tails were small and pointed.

'That happens later, when they grow a bit,' Dan told her. 'These are only a couple of days old.'

'Why are they fighting?' She watched one piglet at the far end being shoved and shooed away by two tougher ones.

'They want more milk for themselves.'

'And why is that one so small?' Hannah pointed to the mini-piglet that had been pushed out.

Dan stopped to take a proper look. 'He's the runt of the litter. There's always one.' He leaned in and scratched Queenie's broad forehead. 'That's a good

girl,' he told her. 'We know they're a handful, but you're doing a great job.' As he stood up again, he told the twins that this was Queenie's first litter. 'She farrowed on Thursday morning, nine piglets in all. It was hard work for her.'

'What's her real name?' Helen drank in every detail. She bombarded Dan with questions, forgetting all her doubts. 'Like, Duke is Duke of Doveton, and Princess is Princess of Cumbria.'

'Queen of the Lakes,' he said proudly.

'What about the piglets? Do they have names?' Helen asked. The little ones squealed and scuffled for position.

'Not yet.' Dan noticed Hannah down on her hands and knees, peering into the far end of the ark. 'What's up?' he asked.

'It's the little one. They're not letting him anywhere near Queenie.' He'd trotted back to try again, but the two bullies had butted him away again.

'Hmm.' Dan made a mental note and stood up.

'Can't you help him?' No wonder the smallest pig wasn't growing as quickly as the rest, Hannah thought. 'Oh, Helen, they're head-butting him and nipping him, poor little thing!'

32

'Best not to interfere,' Dan said quietly.

'Now Queenie's trying to make room for him,' Helen said, as the sow shifted her position. But as soon as a teat was spare and the little pig darted to take hold of it, the others nudged him away. One turned to nip him, another gave a him a quick kick. Soon all the teats were taken again and the runt was left out.

'He's not getting enough to eat, is he?' Helen turned to Dan with a worried frown.

'Probably not.' He glanced up at Duke and Princess, who lumbered towards them.

'What will happen to him?'

Before Dan could speak, Hannah interrupted. 'He's trying again – yes, he's got one! He's having a feed. Oh no, they've shoved him away again!' Her voice rose and fell, then ended with a sigh.

Dan chewed his bottom lip, staring up the hill to the horizon. The ground seemed to rumble and shake as the two pigs plodded down. 'Let's leave him for a day or two.'

'And if he still gets bullied?' Helen asked. She held her breath, afraid that she knew the answer.

There was a long pause. Dan greeted Duke with

slap on his sturdy side and Princess with a friendly scratch. The pigs grunted back at him. 'We'll have to give up on him,' he admitted at last.

'You mean, the little one will starve to death?' Hannah stood up, her face screwed into a frown.

Inside the ark the piglets squealed and shoved.

He nodded. 'It's Nature's way. The big strong ones don't care about the weedy runt, and there's nothing we can do to alter that.'

Still frowning, Hannah clamped her mouth shut. She peered back into the ark.

Helen thought quickly. 'What will you do with the piglets when they're weaned?'

'We rear them until they're a few weeks old. Queenie will stop feeding them before that and they'll be on solid food. I aim to get them ready for the Nesfield Show at the end of the month.'

'Then what?'

'We hope to sell them to other breeders. They have a good pedigree, so they should fetch a good price.'

'Oh!' Hannah interrupted with another running commentary. 'Now they're trying to charge at him. Did you hear that squeal? That was him. They've got him in a corner!'

34

'What's he doing?' Helen dropped on to her knees to look.

'He's fighting back.'

In the far corner, a bundle of pink bodies, snouts, tails and trotters squeaked and scrapped.

'It's four to one!' Helen protested. 'That's not fair!'

'No, but he's brave. He's giving as good as he gets,' Hannah added.

Suddenly the little pig squeezed free. He shot for the exit, running squealing into the open, straight into Helen's arms. She scooped him up and held his panting, bruised body close to her chest.

The other piglets ran out and scattered across the field. Queenie got slowly to her feet. Feeding time was over.

'Poor thing!' Helen whispered. She bent her head to comfort the piglet. 'What will happen to you now?'

Hannah stared at Dan. She couldn't believe there was nothing they could do.

But the farmer shook his head. 'He's a fighter, I'll say that for him. He doesn't give up, do you, sunshine?' He looked uncomfortable. 'But they'll keep on picking on you and you won't get your share of Queenie's milk, will you? No,' he told the twins in the end, 'there's no point hanging on to him much longer. A runt's a runt, and in this tough world they're not meant to survive.'

Four

'Look at his face!' Helen whispered to Hannah as Dan Stott went off to fetch a bucket of food for the grown-up pigs. He assured them that they would be safe with Duke, Princess and Queenie.

'He's smiling!' Hannah cried. The corners of the little pig's mouth turned up, just like a real human smile.

'Isn't he cute?' Helen held him in her arms, where he snuggled against her. All her doubts about pigs had fled the moment she saw this one. 'He's so smooth and soft. And look at his lovely big ears and twinkly eyes!'

'I like his smile,' Hannah insisted. In spite of being kicked, pinched and shoved by the other piglets, he still managed to look happy. 'You're a brave little pig,' she told him.

The runt wrinkled his snout and gave a mini oink.

'See, he knows what we're saying!'

They both loved him on the spot.

'But what will happen to you?' Helen asked.

'Shh!' Hannah warned. 'Don't let him hear that you're worried.'

'He can't understand,' Helen began, but the piglet's ears had drooped and he hid his face against her chest.

'Maybe not, but he knows that something's wrong.' Hannah tickled his neck. He peeped back out at the world. Queenie was grubbing for juicy roots amongst the buttercups, while his eight brothers and sisters ran squeaking and snorting through the clover. Princess wandered nearby, and old Duke rolled over in a patch of dry mud.

'Hannah, you don't think . . . ?' Helen began. She spotted the farmer climbing back over the stile with two heavy buckets.

Hannah shot Helen a quick look. 'Are you thinking

what I'm thinking?' As usual, the twins' minds ran along the same track. 'You've changed your ideas about pigs, then?'

She blushed and nodded, then met her sister's gaze. 'Anyway, what do you say? Shall we ask Mr Stott if we can look after him or not?'

Hannah jumped and skipped round her sister. 'What a great idea. Absolutely brilliant! That's exactly my idea too!' Between them, they could hand-rear the piglet. They could feed him from a bottle until he was big and strong enough to look after himself. If the farmer would let them, they would make sure he didn't starve to death.

Still holding the little pig in her arms, Helen ran to meet him. Hannah was hard on her heels.

'Now then,' Dan Stott said. He realised they were up to something. Steadily he tipped food from one of the buckets into a low trough by the wall. All the pigs, big and little, came running to the sound of breakfast tumbling into the metal trough. 'Stand back, you two, let the dog see the rabbit!'

Quickly the twins stepped aside. It was just as well. Duke charged down the hill, five hundred kilos of galloping pig. Close behind were Princess, Queenie and her eight piglets. The little ones swerved in and out, tumbled and rolled. They ran squealing round the trough while the grown-ups had their breakfast.

They sank their teeth into potato peelings and carrots, leftover bread and biscuits, soggy cereal and pudding. Their heads were down, their mouths stuffed full. Soon the trough was empty.

Forgetting their own little piglet for a moment, Hannah and Helen looked on in amazement.

'They've got healthy appetites, eh?' Dan stood back until they'd finished, then he poured milk into the trough. 'Especially Queenie. She needs extra food while she's feeding her young ones – about five kilos per day, as a matter of fact. That's a heck of a lot of broken biscuits,' he grinned.

The twins watched the three pigs slurp up the milk.

'I see you've kept hold of the little titch,' Dan Stott said as he turned his attention to the runt cradled in Helen's arms.

The piglet squirmed at the sound of his deep voice and tried to hide.

Hannah cleared her throat. 'We'd like to ask you something.'

'To do with Sunny here?' Mr Stott tickled the piglet's chin with his broad forefinger. He gave a slight, sad shake of the head.

'Yes. We'd like to look after him for you.' She came out with it, holding her fingers crossed.

Dan looked steadily back at her. 'Look after him? You mean hand-rear him?'

She nodded. 'We'd do all the work. We know how to feed animals from a bottle. We raised our goat kids, Snip and Snap.' At least, Hannah thought, they'd helped Hilda Hunt at High Hartwell, before the goat twins had come to live at Home Farm.

'And we'd make sure Sunny got plenty to eat,' Helen added. The name popped out. It suited him because of his cheeky grin. 'You wouldn't have to worry about him at all.'

Dan rubbed his chin. 'You'd cycle down here every day for the next couple of weeks, twice or three times a day?'

They nodded. 'Until he's strong enough to take care of himself,' Hannah said.

'You'd have to watch the others. They might not be happy to see him getting special treatment.

'We could build him a pen in one corner of the

41

field,' Helen suggested. She could see that Mr Stott was thinking it over.

'Or keep him in the barn.' This would save the other piglets from getting jealous, Hannah thought.

He sniffed and pulled at the tip of his nose. 'Normally I'd say it wasn't worth it,' he mumbled.

'But you can't let Sunny die!' Helen held him tight.

Dan sighed and picked up the two empty buckets. Three excited piglets ran between his legs and almost tripped him. 'No, you're right,' he agreed. 'OK, let's go ahead and give the little scamp one last chance!'

'Now, you two!' Mary Moore's voice carried a note of warning. 'You mustn't get your hopes up too high.'

The twins had cycled back to Home Farm and burst in with the news. 'We're going to rescue the runt!' Hannah had cried. 'Mrs Stott will give us some of Joe's old feeding-bottles that she doesn't use any more, and we'll feed Sunny ourselves. His mother can't give enough milk for all the piglets, so he gets left out. Without us, he'd starve to death!'

David Moore had listened and nodded. 'Good for you.' He'd turned to Helen. 'When Hannah says "we", does that include you?' he asked.

42

Turning bright red, Helen had to admit that she'd been wrong about pigs. 'They're quite sweet really,' she said.

Their dad had grinned at their mum. But now it was Mary who tried to keep their feet firmly on the ground. 'You can have a go if Dan Stott thinks it's worth it, but it won't be easy. The runt of the litter always has a bad start. He's probably already underweight, and often they don't pick up. In other words, this piglet of yours might not grow up into a proper healthy pig.'

'Sunny will!' Hannah insisted. She was too excited to eat lunch. Early that afternoon they planned to ride back down to Clover Farm and give him his first feed. 'We've decided to keep him in the barn for now. We'll build him a pen and line it with straw. It'll be nice and warm and dry in there.'

'Yes.' Their mum approved of the plan. 'But I still say you shouldn't get your hopes up. Remember, piglets easily get sick when they have a poor start.'

'And one other thing,' their dad said quietly, 'it *is* only a piglet, remember!'

His warning washed over the twins like water off a

duck's back. They ran out to their shed with Speckle and rummaged for bits and pieces to make a piglet pen with. Hannah found some short planks of wood, Helen picked up a length of strong rope. The dog wagged his tail at the excitement.

'Do you want to come, Speckle?' Helen asked.

He jumped up, his pink tongue lolling. They laughed and told him he could if he was good.

'You mustn't scare Sunny,' Hannah warned. 'He's only a teeny-weeny piglet, and you're a big, shaggy dog!'

But they needn't have worried. When they arrived at Clover Farm and Julie Stott came into the yard carrying baby Joe, she was pleased to see Speckle. 'Look, Joe, lovely doggie!' She took him into the house to play. 'Dan's in the barn with the piglet,' she called back. 'One of you can come in and collect the feeding-bottles when you're ready.'

Hannah unloaded the wood from her bike and together they went into the musty barn. They found Dan Stott stacking bales of straw to make three sides of a square. He explained that he'd made a start on building a pen for Sunny.

'Where is he now?' Hannah propped the planks

against a wall. Mr Stott had got to work

'In a cardboard box in the kitchen,' h
'I had to bring him out of the field soon after you
left. The others were giving him a pretty hard time.'

'Is he hurt?' Helen was worried. She helped build
the walls while Hannah used the planks to make a
barrier across the front. She laid them between the
bales a few centimetres apart, then used the rope to
knot them in place. She formed a kind of gate that
Sunny would be able to see through, but not squeeze
past.

'Just a bit bruised.'

'Did he fight back?' Hannah asked.

'That's the trouble. He doesn't give up, even though
the others are twice his size.' Dan Stott stood back.
The pen was ready. 'You can fetch him now,' he
said.

Before the words were out of his mouth, the twins
shot off. They dashed into the kitchen to find Speckle
nudging a white plastic football round the floor with
his nose. Joe clapped his hands.

'You've come for the piglet?' Julie asked with a
smile.

'And the feeding-bottles,' Hannah said.

45

I got a couple ready for you. They're in that bowl of warm water by the sink. It's ordinary cow's milk, so your little pig will need extra vitamins and iron. Give him three drops from this bottle after each feed.' She handed Helen a small brown bottle with a dropper.

They thanked her, anxious to take Sunny to his new home and give him his first feed. Hannah spied a cardboard box on the kitchen table. 'Shall we take him now?'

'Yes, as quick as you can.' Julie picked Joe up to make sure he didn't get in the twins' way as Hannah carefully took the closed box and Helen carried the bowl with the bottles. 'He must be starving, poor little thing.' Julie's soft heart showed in her worried voice.

So they went quickly across the farmyard into the barn, where Hannah put the box gently on the floor. Dan Stott stood by and let her open it while Helen found a comfortable place amongst the hay bales. She held one of the warm bottles, ready to give Sunny his feed.

It was a thin and weak little piglet that Hannah lifted from the box. Sunny weighed hardly anything – maybe two kilos, she thought. He was skin and

bone, and his body was covered in nips and bruises. But his face smiled up at her and he gave a friendly oink.

Helen took him on to her knee. He sniffed at her T-shirt, his snout wrinkling, his small tail waggling. When he smelled the warm milk, he squirmed with delight.

'Here, let me help.' Hannah moved in to tip the bottle towards Sunny's mouth. 'You hold him nice and firm and try to open his mouth so I can pop this in.'

'Ouch!' Helen shook her finger. 'He bit me!'

'Yes, they have sharp little teeth,' Dan said, too late to warn her.

'Wait, I'll try again.' Gently Helen eased Sunny's lips open and Hannah tipped the rubber teat against his gums. He felt the milk trickle into his mouth. He blinked, as if he could hardly believe it – food at last! Then he grabbed the teat between his teeth and sucked greedily.

'Glug, glug!' Hannah gave a sigh of relief as she held the bottle and saw the milk quickly vanish.

Sunny drank and drank until they thought he would burst like a pink balloon.

'That's it, steady on there.' Dan stood, hands on hips, nodding his approval. 'He's got the hang of it all right. Now we have to hope that he puts on weight so he can take care of himself.'

'He will,' Helen promised. She watched the tug of the empty bottle as Sunny sucked on.

'We'll come three times a day if you like.' Hannah gave Helen the second bottle. 'He'll soon be nice and fat.'

'Maybe.' Dan decided to leave them to it. He went outside and climbed into the tractor. But before he drove off he leaned out with a friendly warning for the twins. 'You've done well to get the little chap to take the bottle, but there's still a long way to go.' He eased out of the yard. 'So don't go counting your chickens before they're hatched!'

Five

'Helen-Hannah!' David Moore's voice echoed through the empty house. They were late back from their early morning ride on Solo. It was Monday, their breakfast was ready and waiting on the table, but there was no sign of them.

'Hannah-Helen!' He went out to the barn to check. Solo's tack and saddle were missing, and there was no sign of Speckle. This meant that the twins were certainly not back from their ride.

'Girls!' He stood at the gate, cupped his hands to his mouth and yelled up the fell. His voice echoed, but there was no reply. As he turned to call down the hill, he spied them coming up. Helen rode Solo ahead of Hannah, while Speckle trotted behind. 'Where have you been?' he cried.

They arrived home breathless and excited. Their dark hair had been ruffled by the wind, their cheeks were rosy. Helen dismounted. 'We called at Clover Farm to feed Sunny,' she gasped. This was only their second day of hand-rearing the piglet, but already he seemed more sturdy and livelier than ever. He'd gulped down two bottles of milk and then galloped in and out of the hay bales in the barn, chasing Speckle until he'd tired himself out. They'd left him snoozing in his pen.

'I thought you said you'd do that *after* breakfast,' Mr Moore complained. 'Now your toast has gone cold and the boiled eggs are ruined.'

Hannah followed through the gate with her bike. 'Sorry, Dad. We couldn't resist going to see Sunny. Never mind, we'll take the toast to Clover Farm. Queenie will soon scoff it.'

'That's not the point,' he grumbled. But he was left talking to thin air.

'Sunny had a good night.' Hannah dashed on. She flung her bicycle down by the door. 'We're going to go back soon and weigh him, so we can check how many grams he puts on. Can we borrow the kitchen scales, please?'

Their father watched them vanish into the house. He shook his head. From now on, until the piglet was weaned, the twins wouldn't think about another single thing.

'And can we borrow one of your old cameras?' Helen popped her head back round the door. 'We'd like to take photos of Sunny. Sort of Before and After. Ones when he's the skinny runt, and ones when he's big and strong!'

David Moore sighed then gave in. 'Yes, and yes.' This week it would be all pigs, pigs and pigs! 'Just tell me when to expect you home, will you?'

The twins promised. 'This is important, Dad.' Hannah flung her arms round his neck and gave him a quick hug. 'Sunny's relying on us. And we do want to give him a proper start.'

Helen ran to fetch the camera and came back for her own bike in the shed. 'We want to give him the *very best* start!'

They were already off and speeding down the lane, with Speckle galloping alongside.

'What about your breakfast?' he called. There was no answer. When he went into the kitchen, the toast and eggs had vanished from the table, but not, he knew, into the twins' empty stomachs. They were far too excited to bother about boring things like food.

'Where are those twins of yours?' John Fox asked when he called by with Ben later that morning. 'I haven't seen them around lately.'

'They're at Clover Farm,' David Moore told him. He had his feet up in the sun, snatching a break from his work in the darkroom.

'What's so interesting about the Stotts' place all of a sudden?' The old farmer tipped back his cap and scratched his forehead. He and Ben were missing the twins' company at Lakeside Farm.

'Pigs.'

'You what?' John was ready to take offence.

'Pigs. More precisely, one pig. A piglet called Sunny as a matter of fact.'

John Fox grunted. He revved the engine of his Land Rover, ready to move on. 'I might have known it had something to do with summat on four legs,' he said.

* * *

'Where are Helen and Hannah?' Laura Saunders asked when she rode by the farm gate on Sultan. The black horse looked splendid with his plaited mane and polished tack.

'At Clover Farm, looking after a pig,' David Moore answered from the barn. He was doing the chores that the twins usually did: feeding the chickens, pouring fresh water into the horse trough in the paddock.

'A pig?' Laura was surprised. 'Since when?'

'Since yesterday. You know that they're like when they rescue something. We won't see hide nor hair of them for the next few days.'

Laura rode on alone. The day would seem dead without the twins popping into Doveton Manor to see her and Sultan. Still, if they'd found a pig to look after, she could understand that they must be very busy.

'Where's—?' Sam Lawson dropped by just before lunch.

'Don't ask!' David Moore groaned. 'You're only the third person this morning who would like to know!'

Sam lived down the hill at Crackpot Farm. He was a shy, fair-haired boy in the same class as the twins at school. During the holidays he usually called to see what they were up to. He looked disappointed when he heard they were out.

'They're looking after a pig at Clover Farm,' Mr Moore said more kindly. 'Why not go down and join them?'

'Could do.' Sam blushed bright red at the idea of barging in where he wasn't wanted. He kicked a loose stone across the yard.

'Why don't I drive you down?' The twins' father had finished his jobs for the time being. Before the embarrassed boy could say no, he drew his car keys out of his pocket. 'As a matter of fact, I'd like to see this famous piglet for myself!'

'Two point five kilograms,' Hannah announced. At long last she'd persuaded Sunny to sit still in the scales. The pointer wobbled, then came to a halt.

Helen wrote the figure down in a small green notebook. 'And we just gave him his third bottle of the day, plus his vitamin drops.'

'At this rate you'll soon be big and strong,' Hannah promised him. She checked one of the small cuts on his left side. 'I think this one's turning septic. We should dab some ointment on.'

Sunny wriggled.

'He wants to go down.' Helen closed the book and slipped it in her back pocket.

Hannah lowered the piglet into his pen and watched him settle into a pile of hay. 'He's having a nap.'

'Good.' Helen was tired out. Piglets took a lot of looking after. She stretched out on a row of bales, hands behind her head, staring up at the barn's high roof.

Dan Stott came to look in on his way into the house for lunch. 'How are you getting on?' he asked.

'Fine.' Hannah smiled brightly. 'He weighs two and a half kilos!'

'Very good. At this rate your little tiddler will put on weight faster than any of the others in Queenie's litter.' He strolled on, whistling as he went.

For a while they enjoyed the peace and quiet. Helen stared up at the roof, half dozing. She could hear a tiny snoring noise coming from the pen. Sunny was asleep!

'Helen?' Hannah's voice broke the silence.

'Mmm?'

'Did you hear what Mr Stott just said? He said "*your* little tiddler".'

'So?' The heat had got to Helen. All she wanted to do was relax.

'So, that's what he means – *our* piglet. He's saying that Sunny is ours to keep!' It was what she longed for. 'Who says dreams don't come true?'

Helen raised herself on to her elbows. 'Hang on, Hannah. Just because Mr Stott said "your" doesn't mean he means it that way exactly.' She saw Hannah was running away with the idea that Sunny would one day come to live with them at Home Farm.

'Of course it does.' Hannah refused to listen. She

crouched down to gaze through the bars of the pen at the snoozing Sunny. 'Mr Stott is nice. He means what he says. When Sunny is strong enough, he's going to let us adopt him!'

'We can't be sure.' Helen sat up. Half of her wanted it to be true. Sunny was a live wire, into everything and smiling at everyone. She took her camera and crept across. He lay half-buried in the straw, snoring away. Helen snapped him from this angle and that. 'But it would be nice, wouldn't it?'

Hannah laughed. 'Look at it this way – without us, Sunny wouldn't still be here. Mr Stott knows that. He's leaving us to get on with feeding him while he looks after the others. So when he says "your little tiddler" he already thinks of Sunny as belonging to us.' To her it sounded perfectly straightforward.

'Yes, and if we can help Mr Stott with Queenie and the rest, grooming them and getting them ready for the next show, he's bound to be grateful.' Helen began to see it Hannah's way. 'All we have to do is pick the right moment to ask him when we can take Sunny with us to Home Farm.' She gazed down at him as he slept.

'Yes, but not just yet,' Hannah agreed. 'Let's wait

until Sunny comes off the bottle. That means we can keep on coming down here.' She loved the lowland farm with its meadows and gentle slopes. For the next few weeks their world would revolve around Dan Stott's herd of Large Whites. The summer would roll on, she hoped for ever.

Sam Lawson looked as if he wished he'd never come. Mr Moore had brought him down to Clover Farm, but Hannah and Helen hardly seemed to notice. They went on and on about the piglet – how much it weighed, how clever it was. Anyone would think it was the champion pig of the whole world.

'It's only a piglet,' he told them, standing in the barn door, refusing to go over and look.

Hannah reacted as if she'd been slapped. 'What do you mean, "only"?'

'I can't see that it's anything special.' Sam had grown up in Doveton. It was only people like the twins, who came to live in the country from the city, who thought farm animals were out of the ordinary.

'Sunny *is* special!' Hannah insisted. 'He understands every word you say.'

'Shh!' Helen warned. They'd raised their voices. If

they weren't careful they would wake Sunny.

Sam tutted and turned his back. He went off to find the twins' father in the field where he'd gone with Dan Stott.

Hannah snorted. She was cross. Of course Sunny was different from other pigs – he was brave and curious, and easy to love.

'Never mind him,' Helen whispered when Sam was out of sight. She thought of a way to cheer Hannah up. 'Listen, suppose Mr Stott did mean what he said, and we get to keep Sunny at Home Farm, we have to give him a proper name.'

'Why? What's wrong with Sunny?'

'Nothing. But all the pigs have real names, so why shouldn't he?'

'Yes!' Hannah brightened. 'You're right. What shall we call him?'

Together they went to look at him once more. He still slept, his sides rising and falling with each deep breath, a wisp of straw tickling one nostril. 'Sunshine? Sun Prince?' Helen suggested one or two posh-sounding names. 'Sun Prince the Ninth, because he's Queenie's ninth piglet.'

Hannah wrinkled her nose. Somehow it didn't quite

fit him. Then she had it. 'Sundance,' she whispered, 'because his feet are always dancing in and out of places!'

'That's good,' Helen agreed.

'Sundance the Ninth of Doveton!' From now on, this would be the name of their very own Large White prize-winning pig.

Six

Sundance the Ninth of Doveton turned out to be a
true scamp. As he grew stronger, he was a piglet who
was always on the move. His little trotters danced in
and out of the hay bales in Dan Stott's barn. They
twinkled out into the farmyard and in amongst Julie
Stott's bed of nasturtiums outside the kitchen door.
Hannah would find him there, happily munching the
juicy leaves, one bright orange flower hanging from
his lips, a strand of golden ones settled on his head
like a crown. Sitting in the sun, eating Julie's flowers,
he was the happiest pig on earth.

Then Helen would find him in the kitchen, dashing

under the table, his trotters clattering across the stone-flagged floor. Baby Joe would be crawling after him with a smile almost as broad as Sunny's on his rosy face.

'Now Joe, don't disturb him!' Julie would be wary as the baby approached.

Sunny lay down in Martha's basket in a warm spot by the stove. He blinked and snuffled, and settled down to rest. But as soon as Joe could reach him with his podgy fingers, he would spring out of the basket and dance away on his feather-light feet.

'Don't tease!' Helen scolded.

He darted here and there, sucking up crumbs that had fallen from Joe's chair. Helen would have to chase him out into the yard, where she would find him sitting on Dan's tractor, perched in the driving seat, or smiling down at her from the top of the cab.

'Come here, Sunny!' Helen called him out from behind a wall, under a stone trough, or hiding beneath a pile of straw.

'Sunny, where are you?' Hannah went searching for him to see that he was safe.

But the piglet only came when he smelled food. Three times a day he galloped out of his latest hiding-place and leaped on to one of the twins' laps. He grabbed the bottle between his teeth and the milk was gone in a flash.

By day four of their feeding plan Sunny was able to eat crushed food. They gave him mashed biscuits and cereals, stewed apples and chopped vegetables, as well as his milk. He gobbled it all up. Then they cleaned his dirty face and brushed his silky coat. And they weighed him.

'Four point five kilos!' Hannah announced. Sunny squirmed on the scales, waiting for the treat that he knew would come.

Helen wrote it down. 'Brilliant.' He was putting on weight fast. The cuts had healed, the bruises had faded. Sunny was rapidly becoming the prize pig of their dreams.

But still they didn't pluck up courage to ask Dan if he really meant it when he called Sunny *your* little piglet'. He said it often, with a wink and a smile: 'How's your little tiddler getting along?' or 'What's that little scamp of yours been up to now?' He seemed pleased for the twins when they told him how much weight Sunny had put on, and pointed out that it was thanks to them that the runt of the litter was alive at all. 'If it hadn't been for you two, he wouldn't have lasted beyond Monday,' he said. Now it was Thursday evening and Sunny smiled up at them from the peace and quiet of his very own pen.

Hannah nodded dreamily. 'You're more of a handful than we realised at the beginning, aren't you?' She gazed in at the piglet.

'Oink!' Sunny's lips curled. Hannah could have sworn that he closed one eye and winked.

'How are Queenie's other piglets?' Helen asked. So far they'd been so busy with Sunny that they hadn't found much time to go and visit them.

'Fine.' Dan's slow voice was satisfied. 'We should have them ready for the Nesfield Show. It's only a couple of weeks off now, but the whole litter's coming along well. We'll have them fully weaned by Saturday, and then Queenie can be left in peace. Why not come out and have a look?'

Helen jumped at the chance. Sunny had settled down for his nap, and they weren't due home for an hour. Hannah talked quietly to him. 'Now, Sunny, we're just off to take a peek at your brothers and sisters. You stay here, OK?'

Helen raised her eyebrows at Dan. The farmer

chuckled. 'That twin sister of yours certainly has a way with animals.'

When they climbed over the stile into the pigs' field, the girls recognised big old Duke and friendly Princess. The boar and sow came trundling down the hill. Dan gave them each a wrinkled apple from his pocket and patted their broad sides. Helen scratched Princess between the ears, while Hannah made a fuss of Duke.

'This way,' Dan said, leading them up to Queenie's ark. 'It sounds like feeding time.'

Sure enough, inside the shelter they found the eight fat babies firmly attached to their mother. Four days had made a big difference. Each piglet was round and pink. They had grown to almost twice the size and their straight tails had begun to curl. But they still shoved and pushed while Queenie lay patiently on her side. In the piglet world, they had all to scrap to survive.

'What do you think?' Dan asked their opinion.

'They look great.' Helen noticed which piglet was the boss, which ones took their places lower down. She could see that they were all firm and healthy.

'Will they fetch a good price at the show?' Hannah

hoped that Dan would make a lot of money. She knew that there wasn't much to spare at Clover Farm – the tractor was old, and Dan didn't have much modern machinery.

'I hope so.'

'And can we help you to get them ready for the big day?'

'You sure can. It's the more the merrier, with eight of them to groom.'

'We could come to the show with you, if you like,' Helen suggested.

'And keep an eye on them during the sale?' Dan considered it. 'I certainly could do with two extra pairs of hands.'

'Then the piglets will look their very best,' Helen promised.

He nodded. 'That's an offer I can't refuse. You ask your mum and dad if you can come to Nesfield with me in two weeks' time. If they say yes, I'll make you my official helpers for the day!'

So for the next fortnight the twins worked hard with Dan Stott. Now that Sunny was fit, they began to take him with them out into the field while they carried buckets of food and milk, picked stones out of trotters, brushed mud off backs and wiped dirty faces.

'They're just like babies,' Hannah sighed. One piglet would fall into the mud just after they'd cleaned him. Another would take a tumble down the hill.

'But twice as greedy,' Helen laughed. She watched them race for the trough as Dan poured special food pellets for them. They galloped and leapfrogged to be at the front. Even Sunny crept up to see if he could find a corner to feed from. He sneaked a couple of mouthfuls before the biggest piglet noticed him and chased him off.

'Big bully!' Hannah said. But she didn't worry; Sunny got plenty of special treats. Apples and oranges and other leftover fruit from their mum's café were his favourite, especially banana. Now he ran between her legs to escape from his brother, who ran back to the trough to gobble his share.

'Your young scamp isn't tough enough,' Dan told them. He was enjoying watching the others feed. 'He's as big as the rest, thanks to you, but it looks like you've spoiled him. He's a bit soft compared with his brothers.'

Hannah frowned. 'I wouldn't say soft exactly!'

Helen nudged her. She whispered in her ear. 'Why not ask him now?' They should seize their chance, she thought.

Silently Hannah rehearsed the question 'Mr Stott, is it OK if we take Sunny home with us soon? He's ready to come, and we're longing to have him at Home Farm!' She knew that the farmer would want to know if they'd asked permission, so she'd got this answer ready too: 'Mum and Dad will love it if Sunny comes to live with us. We'll ask them tonight just to make certain, but I'm sure it will be fine.' She and Helen had decided to wait for Mr Stott to say yes

70

before they mentioned it at home.

'Go on!' Helen had voted Hannah to be the one who should pop the question.

Hannah felt her mouth go dry. Finally, as Dan Stott stooped to check one of the piglets, she began. 'Mr Stott, is it OK if—?'

'Boo!' A voice broke in from behind.

Hannah and Helen jumped a mile.

'Sam!' Helen nearly hit him. He'd crept up from the bottom of the field to give them a scare on purpose. He stood there with a broad grin on his freckled face.

'I knew I'd find you here.' He was chuffed that he'd managed to make them jump. 'Talking to pigs, as usual!'

Hannah swallowed hard. She'd almost asked the big question, but now the moment was lost.

'Never mind,' Hannah whispered to Sunny as she took him back to his pen for the night. 'There's no need to worry. Mr Stott knows that you belong to us and that you'll soon be ready to come with us to Home Farm. You just stay there nice and cosy for a little while longer. He's got a lot on his mind at the moment, so we'll just have to wait.' She put Sunny down in his bed of straw. 'Once the show's over and he's sold the litter, that should be a good time to ask!'

Sunny smiled up at her. Nothing worried him, he seemed to say. He sighed and lay flat out. It had been another hard day, getting up to all sorts of mischief.

'Sleep well,' Hannah whispered.

'Talking to a pig!' Sam scoffed again as they rode back up the fell together. He felt left out and cross.

'Better than talking to some *people* we know!' Helen retorted, cycling on ahead.

Now he really was in a huff. He rode his mountain bike off across the field towards Crackpot Farm without even saying goodbye.

After another week of hard work, the twins and Dan were almost ready for the day of the Nesfield Show. The girls went to Clover Farm and learned how to shampoo comb, clip and brush the Large White pedigree piglets. Sunny, too, got the very best treatment. He now weighed a sturdy eight kilos, and when he was washed and groomed he looked very handsome indeed.

For Helen and Hannah the excitement grew as each

day passed. Wednesday, Thursday of the week of the show came and went. Every spare moment was spent pampering the pigs.

'We hardly ever see you,' David Moore grumbled. The twins did their chores at Home Farm and then they would be off.

'Not for much longer,' Helen promised. It was Friday, the day before the show.

'After tomorrow you won't be able to get rid of us.' Hannah had finished her breakfast and was ready to go.

'How come?' Their mum was on her way to work. During the summer months the Curlew Café always kept her busy, but she still had time to find out what the twins were up to.

'That's when we'll ask Mr Stott if Sunny can come home with us.' The answer slipped out before Hannah could stop it.

'Oops!' Helen pulled a face.

'Oh, you will, will you?' This was the first Mary Moore had heard of it. 'Did you know about this?' she asked the twins' dad.

He shook his head. 'No. Sunny who?'

'Sundance the Ninth,' Hannah explained. Her heart

beat fast. She knew she should have remembered to ask nicely.

'Of Doveton,' Helen added. 'He's our piglet.'

'Oh, that Sunny.' It was too early in the morning for Mr Moore. He dipped his knife in the marmalade and spread some on his toast.

'You want him to live here?' Mary looked round her kitchen. 'A pig?'

'-let,' Hannah added, 'A pig-let.'

'Yes, but he soon will be a pig. How big will he be then?'

Helen cleared her throat. 'Just a few hundred kilos.'

'A few . . .'

'Hundred . . .'

'Kilos!' Mr and Mrs Moore looked stunned.

'He won't have to live inside. He can live in the field with Snip and Snap and Solo,' Hannah said.

'In summer, anyway,' Helen thought it was best to tell the whole truth. 'In winter he'll have to live in the barn.'

'What about the smell?' their mum asked.

'Pigs don't smell!' Helen claimed.

They stared at her. 'Oh-ho, so now pigs *don't* smell!' David Moore teased.

'Not much.' She blushed. 'Anyway, Mum, we've been looking after Sunny ever since he was born, just about. He's already like one of the family to us.'

'Along with Speckle, Solo, Snip and Snap, the rabbits, the geese, the chickens . . .' Mary ticked them all off on her fingers.

'So what difference would one little pig make?' Hannah pleaded.

'One *big* pig.' Their mum stared at their dad. He tried to keep a straight face. As usual, the final decision went to Mary. 'What does Dan Stott have to say about it?' she asked.

'Well, we haven't actually asked him yet,' Hannah confessed. 'We're building up to it.'

'Hmm.' Their mother had a twinkle in her eye. 'A pig at Home Farm, eh?'

'A large White pedigree pig!' the twins insisted.

'A pedigree, eh?'

'Mu-um!' Helen and Hannah could hardly bear it.

'Well, why not?' she said at last. 'As you say, what difference is one little Large White pedigree pig going to make?'

Seven

On the day before the show Dan Stott set to work to clean out the trailer which he kept in the barn. He would hitch it to his old Land Rover and drive the piglets into Nesfield. 'It's seen better days,' he admitted, looking anxiously at the patches of rust on the car. 'It belonged to my uncle in the days when he ran the farm. 'Still, once I've given it a clean, it shouldn't look too bad.'

'Nobody will notice.' Julie began to brush out the inside. 'After all, it's the piglets they'll be interested in.'

'Come out of there, Sunny!' Helen called. Their

piglet was getting under people's feet as usual.

He came to her call.

'Hey!' She glanced at Hannah. 'Did you see that? He just did as he was told!'

Hannah tossed back the front locks of her hair. 'Of course.' Super-brainy Sunny understood every word they said.

'Watch out!' Dan was working on the front end of the trailer, trying to hitch it up to the Land Rover. Sunny scampered between his legs. Dan dropped a large spanner on to his foot and cried out.

'Sunny, come here!' Hannah sounded stern. She knew they must train him not to be a nuisance.

He squealed as the spanner clanged to the ground, then he shot into her arms and hid his head.

'Why not take the young scamp out into the field?' Julie suggested.

Helen nodded. 'We'll take the brushes and combs and give the piglets one last grooming ready for the morning.'

So they left the farmyard and climbed the stile. Speckle stopped nosing round the trailer and went too. He bounded over the wall, then watched Hannah climb over with Sunny tucked under her arm. She let him down on to the ground, and the sheepdog and the piglet began to play in the last rays of the evening sun.

One by one Helen and Hannah took hold of each of the eight piglets. They inspected the insides of their soft, silky ears, they polished their trotters, brushed them from nose to tail.

'Now don't go playing in any mud before morning,' Hannah warned. Her arms ached with brushing. 'There'll only be time for a quick groom once we get to the showground.'

They went over each pig one more time, then stood back to admire their work. They all looked beautiful, wandering amongst the buttercups, tails up, ears pricked.

'Oink!' Sunny made a little charge against Helen's leg.

She looked down. 'What is it? What do you want?'

'Oink, oink!'

'He wants you to groom him too!' Hannah laughed.

'You're clean already!' Helen protested. But she picked him up and fussed him. 'Anyway, you won't be going anywhere tomorrow. You'll have to stay here.'

'Oink!' The corners of his mouth turned down.

'Aah!' Hannah went to tickle his chin. 'You want to come too, don't you?'

He waggled his tail at the idea. So soft-hearted Hannah went to ask Dan if Sunny could come to the show. The farmer was still busy. He answered absent-mindedly.

'No problem. We'll see you here tomorrow morning at seven o'clock sharp.' His muffled voice came from under the trailer. 'Don't be late.'

'We won't!' they promised. Sunny was safe in his pen for the night, and the other piglets had settled down in the ark. So the twins said goodnight to Julie and called for Speckle to come. Going home, pedalling slowly along the lanes, their hopes were high. Dan would sell the piglets and they would pop the big question. Tomorrow night they should have Sunny safe at Home Farm.

Saturday dawned bright but windy. Hannah and Helen had planned everything – up at dawn, scramble into jeans and T-shirts, feed the animals. Then breakfast for themselves and out on their bikes by half-six.

'Good luck!' their dad called. He stood at the door in his pyjamas.

'We'll see you there.' Mary Moore was already dressed. She was going to run another of her famous cake stalls at the show. The twins' plan was to cycle down to Clover Farm, then drive across to Nesfield with the Stotts. Their mum and dad would bring Speckle straight there. Eventually they would all meet up at the show.

So they waved goodbye and rode down the hill, through sleepy Doveton. They pedalled hard and arrived at Clover Farm at seven on the dot. Helen's heart raced with excitement, Hannah's hands felt hot and sticky. They both tingled with nerves as they ran into the kitchen to find the Stotts.

But to their surprise, Dan was nowhere near ready. He was standing alone, staring out of the window, deep in thought. He didn't seem to have heard them come in.

Hannah glanced at Helen. There was something about the way he was standing that made him seem upset. Breakfast dishes were still on the table, the plates of scrambled egg almost untouched. Joe's bib and bowl were unwashed, and there were letters scattered everywhere.

Julie came quietly downstairs. She beckoned the twins outside.

'What's wrong? Doesn't Dan realise what time it is?' Helen checked her watch. 'We should be setting off for the show!'

'He's had some bad news, I'm afraid.' Julie herself looked pale and anxious. 'We were expecting it, but not just yet.'

'Is it serious?' Hannah asked.

She nodded. 'We had a big bill in the post this morning. It's for a repair job on the Land Rover, and it's cost much more than we thought.'

The twins were at a loss. They shuffled their feet uncomfortably, still hoping that this wouldn't ruin the show day for them all.

'Dan says there's no way we can afford to pay the bill at the moment.' Julie pressed her lips together. 'Money is a big problem right now.'

Hannah wished they could help. Anyway, she tried to look on the bright side. 'We'll just have to sell Queenie's piglets for a record amount, then!'

Julie looked at her and took a deep breath. 'Yes, you're quite right. There's no point in letting it get us down, is there?' She went back inside to get ready. 'I'll tell Dan you're here,' she called. 'He'll join you out in the field.'

After this they rushed to make up for lost time. Hannah went to fetch Sunny and follow Helen into the field. They rounded up the piglets and waited for Dan to back the trailer in. Then they led them up the ramp. There was a lot of noise – squeals and grunts, oinks and snorts, as Helen tempted them into the trailer with small treats. Meanwhile, Queenie, Princess and Duke stood quietly at the top of the field. When at last the eight piglets were safely loaded, Queenie turned and went into her shelter.

'Ready?' Dan said quietly. He lifted the ramp and bolted it securely in place.

Sadly the twins nodded. Hannah opened the Land Rover door for Sunny to jump in. Quick as a flash he climbed up behind the driver's wheel.

Dan gave a faint smile. 'Has he passed his driving test, then?'

'Not yet.' Helen got in and pushed Sunny gently to one side. They wanted to get away as quickly as possible, knowing that poor Queenie would be lost without her piglets at first.

Helen, Hannah and Sunny squeezed into a space

behind Dan's seat, while Julie sat with Joe in the front. They were ready. All the piglets squealed as the trailer jolted out of the field and up the lane, but they settled down when the road grew smooth.

'Nesfield, here we come!' Julie said. 'And let's hope it all turns out well!'

The twins held up their hands. All twenty fingers were already firmly crossed.

Nesfield Show was much bigger than Doveton. Farmers came from all over Cumbria, Lancashire and Yorkshire to the huge showground by the river. There were four big tents instead of two, half a dozen show-rings for judging the animals, and row upon row of cars parked at the water's edge.

'I don't like it so much,' Helen confessed. 'It doesn't seem so friendly.'

All morning they'd stayed quietly by the piglets' trailer and the crowds had packed in. There were sheepdog trials, and even a television crew to film the competition. Hundreds of tourists came to watch.

'No, but with all these farmers here, someone's bound to give a good price for the piglets.' Hannah's nerves were on edge too. She made sure that Sunny stayed close by, in case he got lost in the crowd.

'We have to wait until twelve o'clock before we can be sure.' That was when the pig competition would be judged. So Helen asked Julie if they could go and look for their mum and dad while she stayed there to look after the trailer. Then they went looking with Sunny inside the big tents. There was a smell of trodden grass and a great crush of people round the stalls.

Soon Hannah spotted their cake stall. It had a big banner saying 'Curlew Cakes', and a long queue waiting to be served.

'Thank heavens you're here!' David Moore gasped as Hannah picked Sunny up and handed him over.

'Hold him tight, Dad. I don't want him to get lost.' She scrambled under the table, glad to be out of the crush.

'Did everyone get here safely?' Mary Moore served a customer and talked at the same time. Speckle sat quietly under the table, keeping out of the way. He wagged his tail when he saw Hannah and Sunny, but he didn't move.

Helen ducked under the table to join them. 'Yes. Julie and Joe have stayed with the piglets down by the river, and Dan is off talking to some other farmers. We have to go back at a quarter to twelve.'

By this time, Sunny had begun to attract attention. Mr Moore sat him on a red cushion in a canvas chair, and for once the piglet didn't fidget. He sat quietly, lips curled into a smile, eyeing the crowd.

'Ooh look, it's a little pig!'

'Aah!'

'Is it tame?'

'What's its name?'

'Isn't he sweet?'

Cries came from all directions.

'Sunny's certainly good for business,' David Moore winked. A big knot of people had gathered to look.

'Look at him, he's enjoying it!' Hannah laughed. Sunny looked like a little prince on his red velvet cushion. She began to relax and enjoy the day.

For an hour or so they served delicious cakes and happily answered questions about their pet pig. They told how they'd rescued him and hand-reared him. They were proud of him, he was a fighter and a cheerful little character. Sunny lapped up the praise. His ears were pricked, he was smiling as he listened to every word.

'You've done well,' Cathy Coates told them. She'd bought her piece of cake and a cup of coffee. Now she stopped for a chat. She and Len were here with their goats, but today they didn't expect to win any prizes. 'It's a much grander affair than Doveton Show,' she explained, 'so the competition's tougher. I hear Dan Stott is still hoping to do well, though.'

'He'll win!' Hannah assured her. 'His piglets are the best Large Whites anywhere. Sunny's one of them.'

Cathy smiled. 'Well, if the rest are like this little one, Dan stands a good chance!'

Sunny oinked, and Helen and Hannah smiled.

'I might have guessed!' Sam Lawson strolled by and stopped, his mouth full of cake. Cathy said goodbye and gave way to him. He came up and stared at Sunny. 'You don't go anywhere without that pig these days.'

'So?' Helen demanded. Sam used to be nice and friendly. Now he was bad-tempered and sulky.

'So . . . nothing!' He turned on his heel with a scornful smile. Soon he'd vanished into the crowd.

'Never mind him,' Hannah said. The queue had tailed off and it was time to go back to the trailer. They called Sunny from his comfy cushion and left the cake stall to their mum and dad.

'Tell Dan good luck!' David Moore shouted. He stuck his thumbs up.

They waved and went out to get ready for the competition.

'Piglet Section!' The announcement came over the loudspeaker. A large crowd of farmers and day-trippers had gathered round the show-ring. 'Litters under eight weeks only. We have ten entries. Your judges are Mr Geoffrey Jones and Miss Hazel White!'

Hannah and Helen herded Dan's piglets into place. They had their own little pen, roped off from the other litters, and the twins wore white coats to show that they were official helpers. Dan stood nearby, keeping a careful eye on things, but it was their job to keep the piglets calm and to pick ones out for the judges to inspect.

'Are you nervous?' Hannah whispered. The judges drew closer, making notes as they went.

Helen nodded. All round the ring they could spot the farmers. These were the men in sensible jackets and wellingtons, with tanned, serious faces. They would pick out the best litters and make an offer once the judges had made their decisions. 'I hope Sunny is behaving himself!' The twins had left him with Julie and Joe, somewhere outside the ring.

'Don't worry. He's on his best behaviour.' Hannah stood to attention as the judges stopped by their pen.

But she spoke too soon. Sunny obviously didn't want to be left out. He must have wriggled away from Julie, and now here he was scrambling between the lady judge's legs and ducking under the rope to join his brothers and sisters.

The judge opened her eyes wide with surprise. For a moment she looked annoyed. 'Is that one part of the same litter?' she asked.

Quickly Helen picked Sunny up and held him tight. The crowd were beginning to smile at the cheeky little pig. He wriggled and waggled his backside, began to snuffle in her pocket for food. 'Yes,' she answered. 'He was the runt. We hand-reared him.'

'Hmm.' The tall woman came up close. 'He certainly doesn't look like the runt. He's in fine condition.' She cast an expert eye over all of the piglets, then she wrote something down on her sheet of paper.

Helen held her breath and glanced at Hannah. Meanwhile, the other judge asked to look at three of the other piglets. He inspected their feet, their mouths, their straight backs and sturdy legs. He nodded, but he didn't say anything. As the judges walked away, the twins closed their eyes and prayed.

At last the judging was over. Each litter was obviously in the running. There were other breeds; black and white Saddlebacks and Danish Landraces. They all looked perfect to Hannah and Helen. How could the judges possibly decide?

Ten minutes passed by. Dan stood talking to three men. He looked serious. The twins bit their lips. Even Sunny seemed to realise that this wasn't time to play games. He nestled quietly in Helen's arms.

Then the judges announced their verdict. Third prize to another litter of Large Whites! Helen saw Dan's face drop. Did this mean that the Clover Farm litter stood less of a chance? Second prize to the litter of flop-eared Welsh pigs. Hannah could hardly bear to listen. First prize to . . . the Large Whites of Clover Farm!

Everyone clapped. Hannah hugged Helen. Julie came running into the ring with Joe and gave Dan a kiss. Dan's smile spread from ear to ear as he shook hands with the other competitors. Then he came over to the twins.

'Brilliant!' he told them. 'Well done!' He was lost for words shaking his head, hardly able to believe it.

'Thank you for all your hard work.' Julie beamed at them. 'You don't know how much this means!'

Helen and Hannah felt tears come to their eyes. They'd done it – they'd won first prize. The Clover Farm litter was the best in three whole counties!

Eight

Of course, many of the farmers at the show were interested in buying the piglets. They came to talk to Dan, mentioning the prices they thought they were worth. Figures flew around. Hannah stood there proudly holding the blue rosette while Helen hugged Sunny.

'Dan will be relieved!' Julie whispered. She let Joe stroke Sunny's head. 'I've never seen him so worried as he was this morning. But if he sells the litter for a top price, we'll be able to pay the garage bill, and then have a little bit left over.'

The farmers still haggled over the price, but things

were looking good. The offers went higher and higher. Two or three of the men lost interest and fell away – the price was too high for them, they said. But there were two farmers left, each determined to buy the piglets. Dan listened and considered the offers. In the end, the younger man stopped bidding, and a tough old farmer was left.

'They're yours,' Dan said with a firm handshake. He looked happy with the price he'd been offered.

'Yes, and I've paid a pretty penny,' the old man grumbled. But he too was pleased. He came across to the pen. 'Still, you have to pay a lot for a good pedigree,' he admitted. 'And these will do nicely. They're good breeding pigs, and that's a fact.'

He began to count the piglets to check that they were all in order. 'One, two, three, four, five.'

Piglets squeezed in and out between the twins' feet. They were bored with the pen, and wanted to eat. They grew noisy and naughty. Sunny looked down from the safety of Helen's arms at the wriggling bodies.

'Six, seven, eight,' the old farmer went on. It was hard to count them if they didn't stay still. 'Where's number nine?'

'No,' Helen began to explain, 'there were only eight piglets for sale.'

'There he is!' The farmer ignored her and spotted Sunny. 'The one with the cheeky grin. That's number nine.'

Helen's mouth dropped open. She turned in alarm to Hannah.

'You don't understand, Sunny isn't included in the litter.' Hannah felt the colour drain from her cheeks.

'Not included?' He frowned. 'He's one of the bunch, isn't he?'

'Not really.' She looked round for Dan. 'Sunny's different. He's been hand-reared. He wouldn't fit in with the rest of the litter if you took him along with them.'

'Well, I made my offer for nine pigs,' he insisted. 'And it's a good offer. I don't want to be messed around like this.'

Julie, who stood nearby, went to fetch Dan. When they came back, they both looked worried.

'Can I help sort things out?' Dan began. 'Mr Sowerby here has bought the piglets, girls. So what's the problem?'

They tried to explain, but they knew that the day

had begun to go disastrously wrong. Dan listened, but he was shaking his head, and the old farmer wore a stubborn look.

'I made the best offer, and you know it,' he said. 'No one else could come near the price I'm giving you. But I'm buying the litter on the understanding that it includes all nine piglets. And if I can't have them all, I won't have any, thank you very much!' He jutted his pointed chin and narrowed his eyes. He wasn't used to being argued with.

Helen and Hannah hated him on the spot. He was a small, wrinkled man with a mean look, they thought

now. He needed a shave, and his tweed jacket was shabby; not the sort of man to look after their lovely piglets.

Dan blew into his cheeks, puffing them out. He towered over the little farmer, but he realised he would have to give in. 'Fair enough, Mr Sowerby, you put in your offer for all nine,' he admitted. 'I'm sorry I didn't make it clear that the runt wasn't for sale in the first place. But now that we've shaken hands on it, I'll go along with you. You can have him included in the same price!'

The twins were struck dumb. Sunny, their beautiful piglet, was being snatched away from under their very eyes. Sunny, the cheeky survivor, the scamp, was not going to come to live with them at Home Farm after all.

Sowerby grunted. 'I'm glad you see it my way. I particularly wanted the ninth one, see. He's a real little character, you can tell that by looking at him.' He went up to Helen and took Sunny away. 'Come on, you young rascal, there's a nice feed waiting for you in the trailer.'

But Sunny had other ideas. He turned his head and gave his new owner a sharp little nip. Sowerby put him on the ground double quick and watched him scamper back to Helen.

'It's best if I drive my trailer up to the ring here,' he told Dan. 'Can you hang on here and keep an eye on them?'

As he went off and began to thread his way through the crowd, Hannah and Helen pleaded with Dan to change his mind. 'Sunny won't be happy if he goes with Mr Sowerby!' Hannah told him. 'The other piglets won't want him. They'll bully him and not let him near the food!'

'Like in the beginning!' Helen said. 'Sunny could starve all over again!'

Dan shook his head. 'Not this time. He's a good, strong piglet now. He'll stand up for himself.'

'It's eight against one!'

'He'll get kicked and trampled on!'

It was no good. 'I'm sorry, girls. You heard what Jim Sowerby said. He wants Sunny, and I've agreed to let him go. There's nothing I can do about it, is there?' Dan shrugged and turned away. He wasn't happy, but there it was. Bills had to be paid, and a deal was a deal. He couldn't get out of the bargain he'd made.

'Jim Sowerby will look after Sunny,' Julie promised.

She could see how upset the twins were. 'He may look a bit mean and cranky, but he's a fine, old-fashioned farmer, and he treats his animals well. These piglets will have a good life with him. They'll live in a big field with plenty of food. There really is no need to worry.'

Helen and Hannah felt awful, but how could they explain? In the end, Dan and Julie couldn't know how much they longed to take Sunny to live at Home Farm with them. After all, the twins had never actually asked. They'd simply dreamed.

Now the bubble had burst. This was real life. Jim Sowerby was striding towards them, explaining something to Dan.

Just then, Sam Lawson walked by. He was the person the twins least wanted to see.

'Where's your piglet?' he asked, back to his old shy self.

Helen pointed to him amongst the wriggling, snorting group. 'Why, what's it to you?'

'I brought him this.' Red in the face, Sam pulled an apple from his pocket. 'I thought he might like it.'

The twins hung their heads. Hannah sniffed.

'I thought you'd be pleased that I'd started being

nice to your pig. What's wrong with you?'

They told him the bad news. 'Dan's sold Sunny,' Helen said. 'He isn't our piglet any more.'

Sadly Hannah took Sam's apple and went to give it to Sunny. She bent down to pick him up. 'We're sorry,' she said softly. 'We never meant this to happen. You're going away with your brothers and sisters to a new home. You have to be a good boy and settle down there. And remember, stick up for yourself if the others try to bully you.' Her voice broke down as she stroked his silky ears.

Sunny put his head to one side. He peered at Hannah. He poked his face towards her to make her look up. Then he gave a sad little squeak.

Dan was coming, so gently Hannah lowered him to the ground.

'Jim can't get his trailer anywhere near the ring because of all the traffic out there,' he told them briskly. 'I've said we'll take the piglets and put them back in my trailer until the traffic thins out. We're just down the hill, so it'll be easier to do it that way.'

Hannah and Helen nodded.

'I'll help,' Sam offered. He was sorry now that he'd always been so rude about their piglet.

So, reluctantly, they each picked up a pig to carry it through the crowd to Jim's trailer.

'There's spare food for them in there, so they'll soon settle down,' Dan promised their new owner. 'Then, as soon as you can drive along by the river here, we'll pop them into your trailer and you can be on your way.'

It was the best they could do in this jam of cars and trucks. Soon the piglets were safe inside.

'Say goodbye,' Julie said softly to the twins as she handed Sunny in to Dan.

'Bye, Sunny,' they said. Hannah patted him, Helen gave him one last stroke.

He didn't go quietly. When Sunny saw that he was meant to go in the back of the trailer with the rest, he squealed. He wriggled and kicked, squirmed and twisted. What was this? Why wasn't he going to ride in the front as before?

Hannah put her hands over her mouth. Helen couldn't bear to look.

'Come on,' Sam said, as Dan made sure that Sunny was firmly locked in the trailer. The piglet still squealed and protested. 'We won't stick around here any longer. Let's go and find your mum and dad.'

Nine

Hannah and Helen felt so miserable that Sam had to explain what had happened to Mary and David Moore. The twins were nearly in tears.

'Sold?' Their dad put down a stack of empty trays which he was loading into the van. 'But I thought Sunny wasn't for sale?'

'So did we.' Hannah knelt on the grass and put her arms round Speckle. The dog leaned against her and gently wagged his tail. Helen was grateful that Sam was doing the talking.

'Never mind,' Mary Moore said. 'It's just one of those things. I'm sure Dan didn't mean to upset you.'

'It's not his fault,' Helen whispered. 'It's ours. We should have left Sunny behind at Clover Farm, then this wouldn't have happened.'

'We should have asked Dan sooner if Sunny could come to live at Home Farm.' Hannah felt tired and hollow. She rested her head against Speckle's soft coat.

'Well,' Mary said, 'help us to pack up here, then we'll go home as soon as we can. I guess this is a day you'd like to forget.'

They dragged their feet to lend a hand. Inside the huge canvas tent everything seemed dull and dismal. The stalls were empty. People went home, leaving litter behind them. Helen, Hannah and Sam stacked boxes at one end of the table, while David and Mary Moore carried them out to the van.

It was almost time to leave, when suddenly there was a small commotion outside the tent. A car horn beeped loudly, there were a few shouts of 'Watch out!' From his quiet place under the table, Speckle's ears pricked up. The twins stopped work and turned to look.

'Try and stop him!' someone cried.

'Impossible! He moves like greased lightning,' someone else shouted back.

'Whoa!'

'Nearly!'

'Oops, missed!' There were sounds of people knocking into one another, little screams of surprise.

Hannah glanced at Helen. 'What's going on?'

Helen put down her load of boxes. 'Something must have escaped from somewhere.' The noise was coming nearer. Whatever it was seemed to be heading for their tent.

Speckle came out from under the table. He listened hard, then trotted towards the exit. The twins and Sam followed. They could hear another noise, the sound of hard feet clattering along wooden gangways. Perhaps they could also hear breathless snorts and grunts.

Hannah's face lit up. She began to run.

Helen followed. They wove in and out of the empty tables, the cardboard boxes, the stuffed litter bins.

'Look out, he's heading for the tent!' There were more cries as still the noises drew nearer. Helen and Hannah raced for the exit.

'Sunny!' Hannah cried, as they broke into the sunshine and open air.

'It is, it's you!' Helen spied his pink face and barrel-shaped body. He raced towards the tent, dashing between legs, jumping over boxes and heading their way. 'Sunny!' She sank on to her knees. He leaped into her arms.

'He's got loose!' Sam came panting up behind. 'How did he do that?' Curious stall holders stopped to look. A small crowd gathered round.

Sunny panted and grunted. He smiled up at Helen and Hannah. He'd found them!

'How did you get out?' Hannah had seen Dan lock and bolt the door to the trailer. All the piglets were supposed to be safely inside.

'I wonder where Dan is?' Sam looked all round. The cars queued to get out of the showground, and hundreds of people still milled about.

For a few moments neither Hannah nor Helen could care less where Dan or Sunny's new owner were. They had Sunny back. They could run away with him, hide him, never let him go away from them again!

But it was Sunny who put a stop to this mad idea. He squirmed free from Helen's arms, planted his trotters firmly on the ground and oinked loudly. His head was down, his snout tilted up, like a dog barking: 'Oink, oink!'

What was Sunny trying to tell them?

'Be quiet, Sunny!' Hannah reached out to hold him back. Other people were moving in, trying to grab the runaway piglet.

Still making a noise, Sunny slipped away between a pair of stout legs. They belonged to a lady who'd been running a free-range egg stall. The piglet swerved away, out of the gathering circle, then he turned to wait.

'He wants us to follow.' Helen was up on her feet and after him. Speckle was the second to react. He trotted after Helen, then turned to wait for Sam and Hannah.

'He's a little handful,' the egg lady smiled. 'You'd better go after him quick.'

So they all ran into the crowd, following Sunny across the empty show-rings towards the carpark where the other piglets still waited in Dan Stott's trailer.

'What does he want?' Hannah caught up with Helen. Sunny kept well ahead of them, galloping down the slope towards the carpark by the river's edge. Everyone turned to watch the chase, amused by the little pig's slippery tricks.

'He's definitely heading for Dan's trailer.' Helen

peered between the jostling crowd. She couldn't see very well. A big horse box stood in the way, blocking their view, but she knew where Dan had parked. 'What on earth is Sunny up to?' Why would he run straight back there?

They raced downhill after him. Farmers stood in pairs and small groups, talking over events of the day, waiting for the traffic to thin out before they set off home. Once, when Sunny vanished underneath a high white van, Speckle bounded ahead and kept him in sight. He showed Hannah, Helen and Sam the way to go.

'Oh no, he's disappeared again!' Sam saw Sunny vanish behind the horse box.

'That's where Dan's trailer is,' Hannah gasped. 'Come on!'

They ran the last few metres, then stopped. There, where the trailer should have been, was a wide, empty space.

'Where is it?' Helen stared at the gap. The grass was flattened, there were other trailers and Land Rovers all around, but Dan's wasn't there.

Sunny snorted loudly. He raced on down towards the fast-flowing river.

'Look!' Sam pointed. The twins peered down the grassy bank. There, teetering at the very edge, its back wheels hanging in midair, was Dan's old Land Rover. 'The trailer's tipped over the edge. It's in the water!'

'Oh no!' They felt their hearts shudder and miss a beat. It was true; the metal trailer with its battered roof had slipped into the river. Water washed round its wheels and up its sides. Still attached to the Land Rover, the trailer was slowly sinking into the mud.

Sunny stopped short at the water's edge. His grunts grew desperate. From inside the waterlogged trailer they heard the terrified squeals of his brothers and sisters.

'They'll all drown!' Sam gasped. He grabbed hold of Speckle's collar to stop the dog from leaping into the river. 'They're trapped in there, and it's sinking fast!'

Sunny stood on the brink, begging them to do something to save the piglets.

'Good boy, well done!' Hannah held on to him. 'Now stay here and don't move!' She turned to Sam. 'You go with Speckle and find Dan. Tell him to come quickly!'

He narrowed his eyes, then nodded and took Speckle back up the slope. He spoke to the dog, low

and urgent. 'Come on, boy, where's Dan? Find him, go on!'

Speckle listened and understood. They raced through the carpark and were soon out of sight.

Then, as the water gushed round the sinking trailer, Hannah and Helen went into action. 'I'll climb on to the Land Rover,' Helen said, 'and I'll try to get in the trailer from this end. There's a narrow gap at the top, look!' The trailer and the car were joined together by a towbar. If this link broke, the trailer would be swept downstream.

'Careful, you might tip the whole thing into the water!' Hannah warned. 'I'll try to use my weight to stop it.' She climbed on top of the Land Rover. 'Now, if you can squeeze through the gap and reach inside, you can hand the piglets up to me.'

Sunny's noisy cries and Helen and Hannah's shouts were all drowned by the sound of the rushing water. Hannah looked round for help, but there was no one nearby. 'Go on, Helen, there's nothing else for it!'

Helen climbed up between the car and the trailer. Luckily she was skinny and tall enough to stand on the towbar and peer in. The trailer tilted and sank a bit further into the mud. But she could see inside now.

Jenny Oldfield

She gasped. The water was already well up the sides. The piglets had crowded to the dry end, but soon the whole floor would be underwater.

'Are they OK?' Hannah called. She could see Helen hoisting herself up and wriggling halfway through the gap as the trailer tipped and sank.

'Wait!' She reached in and stretched to her limit. 'Yes, I've got hold of one!' Hanging on to a drenched piglet, she squeezed out and handed him to Hannah.

He wriggled and kicked out in his panic as Hannah grabbed him, but she held tight. Her plan was to put the rescued ones inside the Land Rover – the only place where she could be sure they wouldn't run away. She jumped down from the roof and opened the door. 'Go in, Sunny!' she told their piglet. He'd watched the rescue, running frantically up and down the riverbank. Now he did as he was told. 'Look after him,' she said. The wet pig shivered and huddled into a corner. Hannah shut the door on them both and clambered back for the second piglet.

By this time, Hannah realised, the horse box had moved off. People noticed the accident to Dan's trailer and came running. They were big men, ready

112

to help. Three of them sat on the front bumper with enough weight to hold everything steady. Now she knew that the trailer wouldn't sink any further unless it broke away from the Land Rover. The twins had rescued piglet number three. Now Helen reached in for the fourth.

'Carry on!' one of the farmers shouted. He sat heavily on the wide front bumper. 'You're doing a fine job. Where's Dan Stott? We need him to try and drive the Land Rover up the bank!'

'He's coming!' From her vantage point on the roof, Hannah spotted Dan's tall, red-haired figure sprinting through the carpark. Speckle and Sam were with him, and behind them was the smaller, stiffer figure of Jim Sowerby. She waved her arms as they drew near. 'Hurry!' Most of the piglets were safe, but if Dan wanted to save his trailer, he would have to be quick. It swayed and creaked, half under the water, dragged sideways by the current.

Helen reached for the next piglet – the fifth. She was soaking wet, her arms ached. But they would do it, they would save them all. Squeezing through the gap once more, she leaned in.

Sam, Speckle and Dan arrived and pushed through

the gathering crowd. Looking grim, Dan weighed up the situation.

'You're lucky these girls came along when they did,' one of the men told him. 'It's their quick-thinking that's got more than half of the piglets out already.'

He nodded. 'I'll turn on the engine and drive slowly up the hill,' he warned the twins. 'Stand clear while I try it!'

'No!' Helen handed a sixth piglet to Hannah, who still crouched on the roof. Her arms were scratched and grazed, her ribs ached. 'Wait until we've got all nine!'

Hannah agreed. 'If you try to pull the whole lot clear, the trailer might break free instead. Then the other three piglets will get washed away!'

'They're right,' Sam told him. 'They know what they're doing, look!'

By this time Jim Sowerby had come gasping up. He saw the danger, looked anxiously at Dan. 'What the heck happened here?' he demanded.

'It looks like the handbrake failed.' It was the only reason why the Land Rover should have rolled towards the river. 'The garage just fixed it, it doesn't make sense.'

Back to their rescue task, Helen reached in for number seven, then eight. Hannah took each one and handed them down to Sam, who eased them into the Land Rover through the window. Inside, the rescued piglets huddled together, drenched and scared, while Sunny sat and kept a careful eye on them.

There was one last piglet trapped inside the dark trailer. Helen could just see him cowering in the dry corner. He squeaked up at her in his terror. Stretching again, crushing her ribs through the narrow gap and bending almost double, she managed to scoop him up. With a gasp and a groan, she pulled him out and gave him to Hannah.

Then, at last, with all nine piglets safe, the girls jumped down to firm ground. Dan squeezed into the cab beside the piglets. He started the engine and put the car into gear. The Land Rover inched forward, its tyres cutting deep into the grassy bank. Everyone stood back with fingers crossed. Mud spurted up from the churning wheels, the trailer lifted and swayed.

'Watch it!' Sam yelled. He saw the trailer break loose. The rushing water caught it and tipped it on to its side. It fell with a great splash, then turned and tipped in the water. Within seconds it was swept away.

Helen and Hannah stood safe on the bank. Jim Sowerby stood quietly beside him. 'That would have been the end of my litter,' he muttered. He went off to fetch his own trailer, shaking his head in relief.

As Dan slowly drove the Land Rover on to level ground, he leaned out and called for bricks or stones to wedge it into position. 'The handbrake's useless,' he told them as he climbed down from the cab. He opened the door a fraction, hoping to keep the piglets safe inside. But one escaped from the huddled group and slid to the ground after him. It was Sunny. He oinked, then ran straight for Hannah, who snuggled him in her arms.

Everyone took a deep breath that all was well, except for one sunk, empty trailer. Julie Stott came running to the scene with Baby Joe. She'd heard about the emergency. Word had flashed round the showground, and soon David and Mary Moore arrived too.

'The twins saved the piglets, every single one!' Sam told them, as proud as if he'd done it himself. 'They were fantastic!'

'You too Sam,' Helen added. 'We couldn't have

done it without you and Speckle.' She felt her face going crimson. There was a broad smile on her face.

'And Sunny!' Hannah hugged him tight. 'He was the real hero. He escaped from the trailer and raised the alarm!'

There would be time to tell the whole story once the excitement had died down. For now, Helen and Hannah stood dripping on the grass, while the farmers carried the nine piglets from Dan's Land Rover into Jim Sowerby's trailer, where it was clean and dry.

Their new owner counted them all in. 'Five, six, seven. You say you just had that handbrake fixed?' He frowned at Dan. 'I'd ask for my money back if I were you. And I'd get them to pay me for a new trailer while I was at it!'

Dan grinned. 'Don't worry, I haven't paid the bill yet.' He had his arm round Julie's shoulder. There was a long story behind that, if anyone cared to ask.

Joe gurgled and clamoured for his dad to hold him. Dan took him and perched him safely on one strong arm. The baby laughed.

'All's well then?' Julie checked that Jim Sowerby was happy.

'Seven, eight . . .' He turned and noticed Sunny in Hannah's arms. 'Number nine!' he recalled. 'The little scamp!'

Once again, Hannah and Helen felt their happiness turned topsy-turvy. Jim was coming towards them, peering through short-sighted eyes. 'Now he's the hero. I said he was a bright little chap, didn't I?'

Everyone who'd seen the rescue agreed that Sunny was the cleverest pig in the bunch.

'He knew just what to do!'

'You should've seen him keeping the others in order.'

'Wasn't he the one who raised the alarm in the first place?'

'He did. He deserves the blue ribbon all to himself!' Jim Sowerby smiled and drew the shiny rosette from his pocket. He clipped it securely on to Sunny's ear. 'He's the champion piglet of all time!'

The twins felt torn in two. They were so proud of Sunny, yet so sad they must lose him.

Mary Moore came softly up. 'Say goodbye, girls. It's time for Sunny to go.'

Slowly Hannah held him out for Mr Sowerby to take. Sunny wriggled. He didn't want to leave them.

'Nay.' The grizzled farmer shook his head. 'I've got eight healthy piglets in my trailer thanks to you. I'm keen on this ninth one, it's true. I reckon he's going to make the best pig of the bunch in the end. He's a handsome little fellow, and full of cheek.' Gently he stroked Sunny's head. The blue rosette fluttered in the breeze. 'But I can't take him away from you, not now.'

The girls gazed at the farmer with their big brown eyes. Was this true? Could Sunny come to Home Farm after all? Hannah took him back. Helen bit her lip and glanced at her mum and dad. Sam stood in the background with Speckle and the Stotts.

Jim Sowerby gave a short, sharp nod and stepped back. 'Aye, take the runt home with you,' he decided. 'I reckon you all deserve it.'

Another Hodder Children's book

SOCKS THE SURVIVOR
Home Farm Twins 8

Jenny Oldfield

Helen finds a litter of abandoned kittens.
Night and day the twins nurse and feed
them – but the kittens are weak, and
Hannah's sure one of them is sick. Will
the kittens pull through?

STEVIE THE REBEL
Home Farm Twins 9

Jenny Oldfield

Stevie's a donkey looking for a home. The twins meet him at a local donkey sanctuary and long to make friends with him. But he's bad-tempered and vicious, and it's hard to get near him. What has happened to Stevie to give him such an attitude? Helen and Hannah aim to find out – because unless they can tame him, he'll *never* find a home!

SAMSON THE GIANT
Home Farm Twins 10

Jenny Oldfield

Samson is an Old English Sheepdog in need of some exercise! He lives in town with his owners, and they're too busy to take him out. Helen and Hannah are happy to help, and soon they're walking him every day. But when they take Samson to Home Farm for a day, things go terribly wrong, and he disappears, badly injured. Can the twins track him down?

ORDER FORM
HOME FARM TWINS
Jenny Oldfield

0 340 66127 5	SPECKLE THE STRAY	£3.50	☐
0 340 66128 3	SINBAD THE RUNAWAY	£3.50	☐
0 340 66129 1	SOLO THE HOMELESS	£3.50	☐
0 340 66130 5	SUSIE THE ORPHAN	£3.50	☐
0 340 66131 3	SPIKE THE TRAMP	£3.50	☐
0 340 66132 1	SNIP AND SNAP THE TRUANTS	£3.50	☐
0 340 68990 0	SUNNY THE HERO	£3.50	☐
0 340 68991 9	SOCKS THE SURVIVOR	£3.50	☐
0 340 68992 7	STEVIE THE REBEL	£3.50	☐
0 340 68993 5	SAMSON THE GIANT	£3.50	☐

All Hodder Children's books are available at your local bookshop or newsagent, or can be ordered direct from the publisher. Just tick the titles you want and fill in the form below. Prices and availability subject to change without notice.

Hodder Children's Books, Cash Sales Department, Bookpoint, 39 Milton Park, Abingdon, OXON, OX14 4TD, UK. If you have a credit card you may order by telephone – (01235) 831700.

Please enclose a cheque or postal order made payable to Bookpoint Ltd to the value of the cover price and allow the following for postage and packing:
UK & BFPO – £1.00 for the first book, 50p for the second book, and 30p for each additional book ordered up to a maximum charge of £3.00.
OVERSEAS & EIRE – £2.00 for the first book, £1.00 for the second book, and 50p for each additional book.

Name ....

Address ....

....

....

If you would prefer to pay by credit card, please complete:
Please debit my Visa/Access/Diner's Card/American Express (delete as applicable) card no:

Signature ....

Expiry Date ....